SOPHIE GUERRIVE

DINOSAUR DETECTIVE'S

SEARCH-AND-FIND RESCUE MISSION

WIDE EYED EDITIONS

THE OLD TOWN

DINOSAUR DETECTIVE!
CAN YOU HELP?
MY BEST FRIEND CAT
HASN'T COME HOME.
HE'S WEARING A
BLUE COLLAR WITH
A GOLD TAG.

I'M ON THE CASE!

DINOSAUR DETECTIVE
ALSO NEEDS TO FIND:

- A MAN WITH AN AXE
- A CAMEL
- TWO FRIENDS ON A BENCH
- A FIREFIGHTER

DINOSAUR DETECTIVE! PLEASE HELP ME! MY BLUE TOAD JUST LEAPED INTO THE AIR AND NOW I CAN'T FIND HER!

TOAD-FINDING MODE ACTIVATED!

BZZZ

DINOSAUR DETECTIVE ALSO NEEDS TO FIND:

- A STRING OF PEARLS
- AN ANT TAKING A BATH
- A SLEEPING BEAR
- A WATERING CAN

THE MOUNTAIN

DINOSAUR DETECTIVE! ONE OF MY STUDENTS IS HIDING BECAUSE HE HASN'T DONE HIS HOMEWORK. CAN YOU FIND HIM?

CONSIDER IT DONE, SIR!

DINOSAUR DETECTIVE ALSO NEEDS TO FIND:

- A WOMAN DIVING
- A MAN WITH A YELLOW FLAG
- A BARKING DOG
- TWO SKIERS HOLDING HANDS

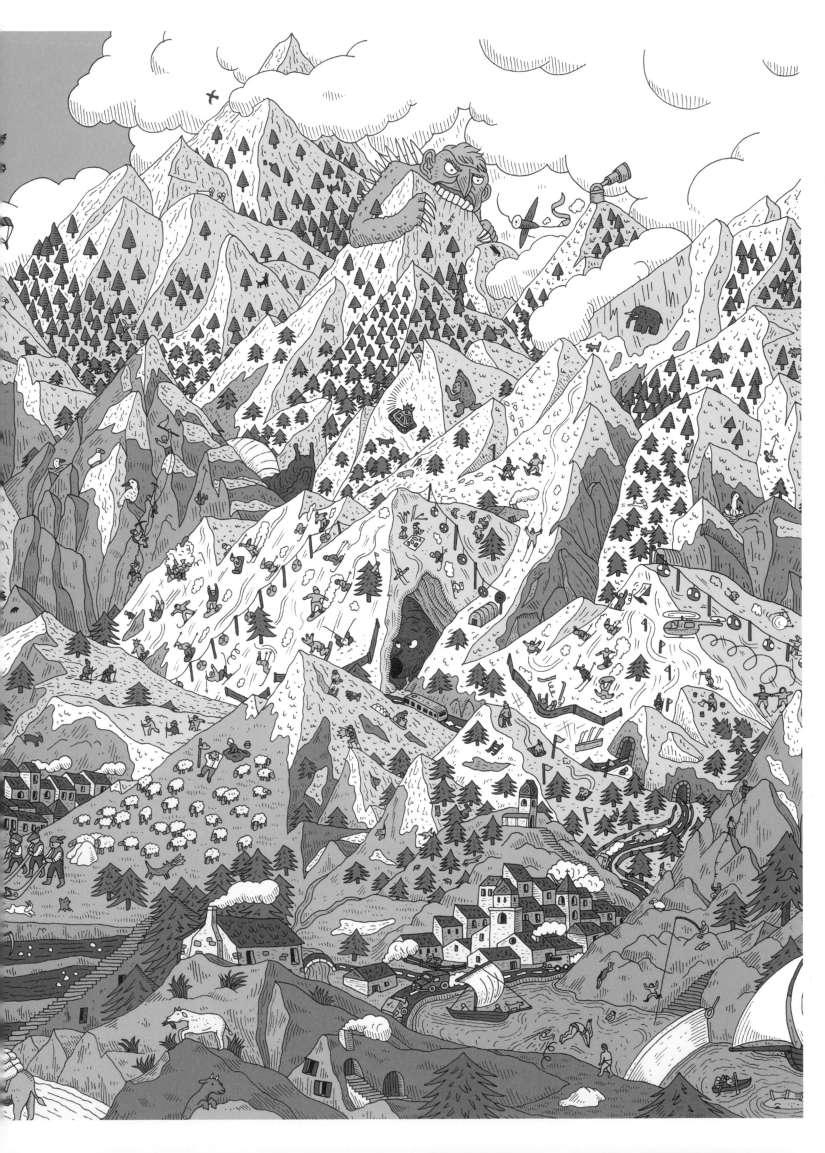

I'VE LOST MY FRIEND, SNAKE. SHE MUST BE SOMEWHERE IN THE FAIR.

PLEASE HELP ME FIND HER!

SURE THING!

DINOSAUR DETECTIVE ALSO NEEDS TO FIND:

- A WALKING BANANA
- A WIZARD
- A COW WEARING A GREEN DRESS
- A SKELETON IN A TOP HAT

DINOSAUR DETECTIVE! CAN YOU HELP ME FIND MY RABBIT? HE ESCAPED WHILE WE WERE DOING GYMNASTICS ... HE COULD BE ANYWHERE!

I'M ON THE WAY!

DINOSAUR DETECTIVE ALSO NEEDS TO FIND:

- AN ELEPHANT
- A SPRINTER IN A YELLOW T-SHIRT
- A MAN WALKING A BROWN DOG
- A GOLD-MEDAL-WINNING HORSE

THE MUSEUM

I CAN'T FIND MY GRANDPA! I DON'T KNOW THE WAY HOME ON MY OWN! HELP ME, DINOSAUR DETECTIVE!

OH! NO PROBLEM!

DINOSAUR DETECTIVE ALSO NEEDS TO FIND:

- A FROG IN A BOW TIE
- A VAMPIRE
- A LOST BOOK
- A MAN WITH A BROKEN ARM

THE FOREST

DINOSAUR DETECTIVE, CAN YOU HELP? MY SON HAS LOST HIS WAY AGAIN. HE IS SO ABSENT-MINDED! CAN YOU FIND HIM?

OFF I GO!

DINOSAUR DETECTIVE ALSO NEEDS TO FIND:

- A HUNGRY UNICORN
- THREE BABY BIRDS IN A NEST
- A WOMAN READING
- A GRINNING CAT

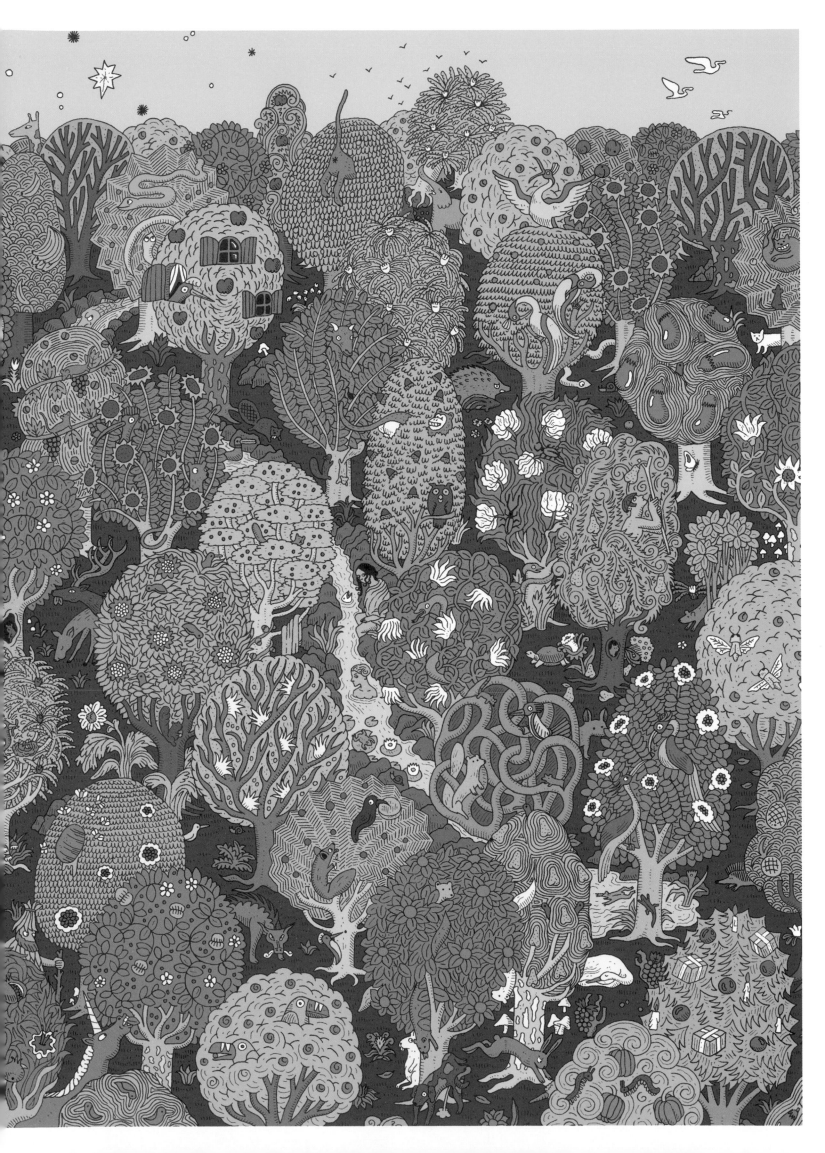

SPACE

MY BOSS HASN'T COME BACK FROM HIS BUSINESS MEETING, WHICH IS WEIRD, BECAUSE HE'S ALWAYS ON TIME! CAN YOU FIND HIM, DINOSAUR DETECTIVE?

TRANSFORMING MY PLANE INTO A FLYING SAUCER!

DINOSAUR DETECTIVE ALSO NEEDS TO FIND:

- A ROBOT WITH AN UMBRELLA
- A GREEN FLAG WITH A CROSS ON IT
- SOMEONE IN BED
- A CHICK HATCHING FROM AN EGG

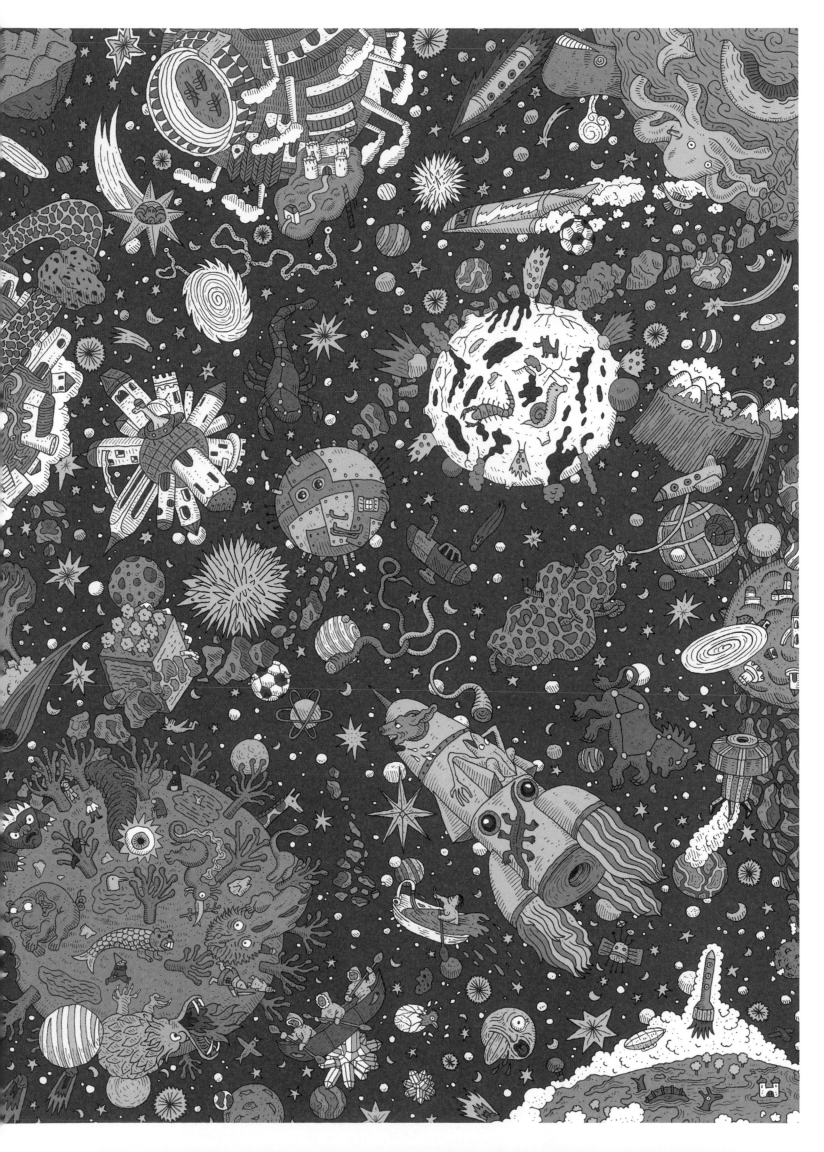

THE OCEAN

MY HUSBAND WENT SAILING AND NEVER CAME BACK! PLEASE BRING HIM HOME!

AT YOUR SERVICE!

DINOSAUR DETECTIVE ALSO NEEDS TO FIND:

- A MAN FLYING A KITE
- A BEACHED WHALE
- A GIANT PINK-AND-PURPLE JELLYFISH
- A SEA MONSTER HOLDING AN OAR

THE OLD TOWN

THE FAIR

THE CAVES

THE OLYMPIC VILLAGE

THE MOUNTAIN

THE MUSEUM

THE FOREST

THE OCEAN

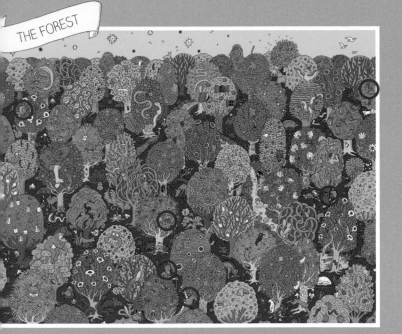

SPACE

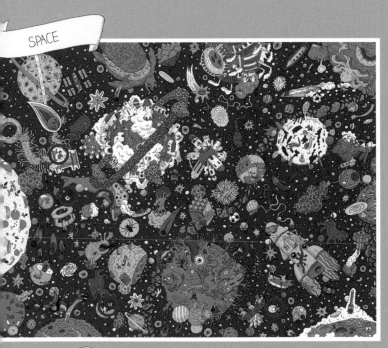

THE BIG CITY

THE JUNGLE

HOME

First edition 2017
Published with the permission of Comme des géants inc.,
6504, av. Christophe-Colomb, Montreal (Quebec) H2S 2G8
All rights reserved
Translation rights arranged through the VeroK Agency, Barcelona, Spain
First published in the English language in 2017 by Wide Eyed Editions,
an imprint of The Quarto Group,
The Old Brewery, 6 Blundell Street London N7 9BH
QuartoKnows.com
Visit our blogs at QuartoKids.com

Important: there are age restrictions for most blogging and social media sites and in many countries parental consent is also required. Always ask permission from your parents. Website information is correct at time of going to press. However, the publishers cannot accept liability for any information or links found on any Internet sites, including third-party websites.

ISBN 978-1-78603-071-9

Illustrated in pen and coloured digitally
Set in Claire Hand

Designed by Karissa Santos
Edited by Kate Davies
Published by Rachel Williams and Jenny Broom

Manufactured in Dongguan, China TL012019
5 7 9 8 6 4